A Letter to Claudia

By Barbara Avon

A Letter to Claudia

The Sequel to Q.W.E.R.T.Y.

Written by Barbara Avon

All rights reserved.

No part of this book may be reproduced or transmitted in any form or by any means, electronic or mechanical, including photocopying, recording or by any information storage and retrieval system, without written permission from the author, except for the inclusion of brief quotations in a review. For permission requests, write to the publisher, at the E-mail address below to the attention of Barbara Avon:

barbaraavonauthor@gmail.com
www.barbaraavon.com

All of the characters in this book are fictitious and any resemblance to actual persons, living or dead, is purely coincidental.

Copyright © March 2021 by Barbara Avon
First Edition Printed 2021

Twitter: @barb_avon
Cover Design by Barbara Avon
Original Front Cover Photograph Credit: Jenny Hayut

Acknowledgements

To David Denewett, Author, and Creator of "Storytime with Og" – for your friendship, and kindness. Keep telling stories. The world needs them.

To Jenny Hayut, Poet, Author, and Photographer – thank you for allowing me to use your photo on the cover.

To my family who supports me in every way possible – thank you.

To my husband – my everything.

Note: Some scenes depict dark, and sensitive themes.

It is only in the depths of sleep, that my yearning for you is realized. In my dreams, music envelops us. We drift on the notes towards a magical place where there is no sorrow or longing. You are majestic, and radiate a love so pure, I fail to remember you are gone.

One
October 1972

I followed you on a Tuesday, masked beneath my own face. You poured me stale coffee from the decanter as I sat in your parents' diner, drooling like a Goddamn kid in lust. The guy at the end of the bar stole your attention and I wanted to pummel his face into an unrecognizable mass soiling his pink polo shirt. ~~*Who the fuck wears pink?*~~ *My pen moved furiously, as I pretended not to listen to you tell him you were going to the Fair. You always hated the Fair, Claud…I fucking hate the Fair…*

Luke stood at the Fortune Teller machine feeding it quarters and stalking his wife, who had been resurrected by the keys of a warped Remington typewriter barely a month ago. Every night, he gets on his knees and prays to the machine, seeking guidance from a hunk of metal, and every morning, he drowns in Whisky, to stave off the urge to tell the world that his haunted typewriter makes everything he types come true.

A year earlier, he had witnessed her untimely death, and fueled by a deep love for her, he made it so that they had never married. The Grim Reaper had taken a detour.

For weeks, Luke imagined reuniting with her by starting over, wooing her into submission under his fake name, and despite the fear that choked him with each breath, he had mustered enough courage to step foot through the diner door and gaze upon a once-dead woman who knew him only as "Paul". He had listened intently to the cadence of her voice, trying to find a coded message in her words. With the knowledge that she was planning a trip to the local Fair, Luke had tossed a five-dollar bill on the counter and made his way down country roads like a Dick in layman's clothes.

"You might want to try sweet talkin' that thing."

"What?"

"The fortune teller."

"Oh. Yeah."

"You followin' me? First the hospital, then at Pop's, and now here."

He thought about how he had written himself back to the hospital waiting room where they had first met and adopted a fake name. Luke stared behind her at a circle of girls who all wore the same miniskirt in colours that made his eyeballs bleed. Pink Shirt guy towered a foot above them and was sending invisible daggers Luke's way.

"Do you…want me to follow you?"

"I thought you said you have a girlfriend?"

"I do," he lied.

"That's what I thought. Good to see you're healing nicely, Paul," Claudia said, stroking his cheek with one thumb before walking away.

"Claudia, wait."

"How do you know my name?" she asked, twisting half her body towards him -- the half that had been crushed by a semi's front end.

"Heard it at the diner."

"Oh. Well, what do you want?"

"I…nothing. I wanted nothing."

"You sure?"

"Yeah."

"See you around."

"Fuck," he whispered, watching her join her coven. He kicked at the dummy in the machine who grumbled in response.

His heart ached, and he clutched at it dramatically as he pushed his way through the crowd, stepping on little toes, and ignoring the dirty looks given to him by angry parents.

In the parking lot, he leaned against his pick-up, and cried openly, sickened by the unfathomable truth that she would never know him as the man who pledged his forever love.

He drove home too fast, filling his lungs with cancerous streams of heaven. Reaching over, he pulled a flask from the glove compartment and suckled the thing until he felt light-headed. The snot dripped from his nose and he wiped at it, remembering their wedding day when icing had lined Claudia's upper lip and he kissed it away, tasting her beneath the sweetness.

Pulling into his driveway, he stared at his house - their house - that felt like a crypt without her. Knick-knacks had been put away after the last of the earth was thrown over her grave. Mementos of their lives together now sat in the basement, buried along with her corpse. He had visited the cemetery after her rebirth, drunk, and high. Luke spent an entire afternoon searching the grounds, but the marker had disappeared, along with what little was left of his sanity.

Darkness enveloped him. The house was cold, despite the humidity that lingered in the air. Parched, he walked to the kitchen and filled a tumbler full of whisky. It was his soul that was parched, and not his throat where he often imagined the hangman's noose tightening and ending the charade, he called his life.

In the living room, he stood in front of it like a worshipper standing before a false idol. The Remington exuded something preternatural, and as if he had swallowed a handful of magnets, he was drawn to it.

He sat down carefully, cautiously. Taking one long gulp of liquid courage, he placed his fingers on the keys. Booze rose to his throat as he recalled his past life, and his ambitions as an author. She had been so proud of him; his number one fan. That dream had died when she died. Yet, there were moments when the words called to him, and his fingers merrily danced:

How serene they looked, languishing in the grass. With cherubic faces and fingers clasped, it was as if they came alive beneath a masterful brush stroke. There was no breath left in either of them. The berries were wild, and poisonous; the fruit as blue as their lips.

Panic seized him as he erased the words…

How serene they looked, languishing in the grass. With cherubic faces and fingers clasped, it was as if they came alive beneath a masterful brush stroke. There was no breath left in either of them. The berries were wild, and poisonous; the fruit as blue as their lips.

"Jesus Christ, that's all I need, is two dead kids in the house," he said out loud.

The chair creaked as he leaned back with a smoke between his lips. He struck a match on the antique desk and staring at the flame, he saw different flames. They were the ones a painted dragon vomited as it graced the entrance way to the fair grounds. His desire was manifested in those flames, and closing his eyes, he remembered their words:

"You might want to try sweet talkin' that thing."
"What?"
"The fortune teller."
"Oh. Yeah."
"You followin' me? First the hospital, then at Pop's, and now here."

Opening his eyes, he typed frantically:

"What if I was?"
"What? Following me?"

"Yeah."

"What about your girlfriend?"

"We split."

Luke stood abruptly making his chair topple to the hardwood. Ash fell from his smoke, and as he stared at it drifting towards his sneakers, hardwood was transformed into grass, and her sweet, delectable, scent wafted towards him.

"That bad, eh?"

"What do you mean?" he asked, staring up at her.

"You couldn't even look at me when you said that. She broke your heart?"

Marital vows drummed in his ears.

"Paul? Your smoke's out."

"Yeah," he said, tossing the butt underfoot. "Listen, how about a ride?"

"What?"

"On the Ferris Wheel. We can talk."

"Talk."

"Or not. Doesn't matter. We can just sit. The great thing about it is, you don't have to know which way you're headed. You just have to get on and enjoy the ride."

"Practicin' your poetry, again?"

He shifted uncomfortably, unable to read her. "How about a drink, then?"

"You're a little fucking late. Connor would flip out."

"Who the fuck is Connor?"

"Over there," she said, pointing to Pink Shirt guy. "Good to see you're healing nicely," Claudia said, stroking his cheek with one thumb before walking away. "See you around!" she cried behind her.

Her words sent him back, jostling him through time. At home, sprawled across the floor, Luke lied motionless. A cicada shrilled in his ear, admonishing him for his stupidity. Lifting only one finger, he scratched his initials in the wood inside a crudely drawn heart; a lover without a mate.

Two

I tried to take you home with me, baby. I swear on my life. Each time I tried, the transport came barrelling towards you – its headlights like eyes, its grill snarling. Now you stare at me through a stranger's eyes, and it's a fate worse than death.

Luke was on his belly, picking lint from the area rug and creating a tiny pile reminiscent of an anthill. Pressing the fibers with his thumb, he felt like an omnipotent being, capable of destroying an entire world.

An invisible puppeteer forced him to his hands and knees, and he performed ten awkward push-ups. Stretching his legs out, he attempted a traditional push-up, but his arms buckled, causing him to sit up and light a smoke in defeat. Pink Shirt guy laughed incessantly from another dimension; thick arms bulging beneath his shirt sleeves.

Disgusted, Luke sat at the antique desk and with the clanging of a few keys, he left his earthly body on the floor:

We travel beyond the city limits, to the place we last met. The Ferris Wheel sits frozen; its steel garters, rusted. Youthful cries are suspended on air. The majestic carousel has ceased its endless ride to nowhere, but our love, it spins eternal.

The snow coated his hair and shoulders. His breath was visible before him, emitted in small, quivering puffs. In the distance, he saw a mishappen form sitting on a dilapidated bench. Her red coat was like a bloody blob against the backdrop of white. A mop of blue curls was hidden beneath a yellow beret, and at her feet, a large wicker bag sat open collecting the crystals as they fell from the sky.

Luke stared at his hands. His veins emptied; the flow interrupted by the knowledge that there would be no victor in this game of chance. Stuffing his hands in his trench coat, he walked towards her, and as he stood in front of her, he presented himself as an ally.

"Damn cold, isn't it?"

She shaded her eyes with one hand and looked up at the stranger. "I think it's nice."

"Do you mind if I sit with you?"

"Please," she said, scooting over.

Luke brushed the snow from the bench and sat down. They both looked at the dead Carnival, painted in vintage hues. Notes from a lamented organ drifted towards them.

"My name is Luke."

"My name is Claudia."

"That's a pretty name."

She blushed. "Thank you. Are you here alone?"

"No. I'm here with you," Luke said, charming her. "What about you? Do you have children, Claudia?"

She looked away, watching pretend girls and boys play in the snow. "She was the dream that never came true. I never had the chance to be a mother." Facing him once more, she asked, "Do you have any kids?"

"I wanted to. My wife…she died young."

"I'm so sorry."

Luke felt alien in his new body. An uncontrollable cough overtook him, and he accepted a handkerchief from his old friend.

"What's the difference between 'like' and 'love'?" he asked when he was able to speak.

"One is pleasant. The other, painful."

He raised an eyebrow at her. "That's very poetic."

"Did I win a prize?"

"Well, no. The answer is that two letters are the difference."

Claudia stared blankly before dissolving into laughter. "You are funny."

"I'm glad you think so. Say, what's in the bag?"

"Nothing," she said, staring at it briefly. "I like to carry it around. Just in case."

"In case?"

"To carry things home."

"I see. Which one was your favourite?"

"Excuse me?"

"Over there," he said, pointing with a gnarled finger. "Which ride was your favourite?"

"Oh," she said, embarrassed. "That would have to be the Ferris Wheel."

"Any particular reason?" he asked, placing one hand over hers.

She gazed ahead of her, wrinkled cheeks blushing a subtle cerise. "You don't have to know which way you're headed. You just have to get on and enjoy the ride."

"Yes," he said, fighting back the tears. "I like that."

Swiftly turning her head, she looked him dead in the eyes, "Someone special once told me that, but…"

"But?"

"But I can't remem…"

"Claudia?"

"How do you know my name?"

"You just told it to me."

"No, I didn't! Who *are* you?"

"I just said it. My name is Luke."

"Luke?"

"Yes. That's right."

The silence was thick; foreboding. Claudia wrung her hands together nervously.

"I have to go now, Luke."

"Claud, wait! I mean, don't go, yet." He chuckled, "You look like my late Nonna, wringing your hands together like that. Except, she always had a rosary threaded between her fingers."

"I know," Claudia said, before melting into a red, gloppy, puddle, "she's sitting right beside you."

Somewhere in a nearby tree, a bird squawked in time with the organ.

Three

The canine sniffed at the tire of Ricky's 1968 lime green Chevy Nova. Smoke stuck to the interior of the car, and on Luke's sweaty face. One foot was propped against the dash, causing his fatter cousin all kinds of angst.

As kids, they had been inseparable, mostly because their Italian mothers were the God-fearing type and Heaven forbid that either one of their children would get the wrong idea from the neighbouring families.

"They make pasta using powdered cheese!"

"That's nothing. One buffone *likes to suntan naked. Right on the front lawn!"*

"Mrs. Windfied?"

"No! Mister *Windfied."*

"Sacrilegio!"

Luke swished the whisky in the half-empty bottle. The effects of his marijuana joint were curative, relieving him of the disease that had wreaked havoc on his mind. Love was a curse, and his heart sat on a shelf right next to the peach preserves, enclosed within a jar, still pulsating.

"Well?"

"Well, what?"

"You're high, man."

"That's the point."

"I asked you what the fuck we're doing here. And get your stinkin' feet off my dash, asshole."

"How's Sandra? Bang her yet?" Luke asked, ignoring his request.

"Don't you fucking talk about her that way!"

"What? You in love, or something?" Luke laughed, which earned him a punch in the arm, bruising his ego.

"Yeah. I think I am."

A homeless person resembling a zombie shuffled towards them. Luke rolled down his window causing a stream of smoke to drift towards Heaven. He tossed a five-dollar bill at the man and it floated like a badly built paper airplane. Reaching into his faded Levi's, he tossed a twenty-dollar bill, and then a fifty-dollar bill, until homeless man stood at the window like a kid trick-or-treating.

"That's all I got," Luke told him, rolling up the window and smashing his fist on the lock.

"Jesus. You *are* high," Ricky said, bemoaning the lost cash.

Luke took a swig of whisky and stared across the street at the house with pale yellow siding. The red paint was peeling on the front door after years of neglect. Last Summer, he had taken a brush to it, but that Luke didn't exist anymore. The front curtains were wide open, and he could see Claudia's mother clearing the dishes from the dining room table. He thrust the bottle towards the woman, engaging in a one-sided cheer, "Salute."

"Oh, for crying out loud. What are we doing here!?"

"See that woman?"

"Yeah. So?"

"She's my mother-in-law."

"What the hell are you talking about?"

Luke's insides gurgled. He was surviving on booze instead of food, but no matter how much he drank, her angelic likeness was before him, sprouting horns. His wife had become a tease.

"Remember after Zia's funeral, you showed up with that rusty old typewriter?"

"It was only last month, stupid."

Luke nodded, accepting the moniker.

"The typewriter…it's possessed or something. I asked Ma if Zia was a witch, and she had a fit. I'm thinking it's the typewriter. It's magic, or…I don't know, but it makes things come true."

"Come true…how?"

"Is there more than one way?"

"No, I mean, what happened to make you think that?"

Bile rose to Luke's throat, forcing him to open the car door and leaning over, he gagged until his throat felt raw.

"You going to puke?"

"No," he said, slamming the door shut. "You won't remember her, because I made sure we never got married, but I had a wife," he said, wiping at his mouth with the back of his hand. "She…died. Suddenly. I used the typewriter to try and bring her back, but she always ended up dying. I couldn't take it anymore. I went back to where we first met and pretended I had a girlfriend. After that, she was okay. Claudia's okay. But she doesn't know me anymore, and…"

"Oh, I get it! This your new book?"

"No. Fuck, are you listening, or what?"

An alien glow blinded them. Using his windbreaker, Ricky cleaned the front windshield of the fog, sullying his new jacket with smoke stains. A woman wearing bright, white, knee-high boots walked on the opposite side of the street. Luke stared at her like a man deeply in love. Had he been close enough, he would have seen his reflection in her eyes grow dimmer.

"That's her," he whispered, nudging Ricky who was

busy spitting on his jacket to clean it.

"The wife?" Ricky asked, howling. "Hey! Where are you going!?"

Luke stumbled out of the car and met the grass, face first. Oblivious to the grass stains on his knees, he blew into his hands to smell his breath, losing his words on the night air. They met at a proverbial crossroad.

"Cristo! Again? What is your problem?"

"Hi," he managed to say.

"Hi? You're acting like a crazy person. Come this way before Ma sees you."

He followed her as she turned on her heel and walked to the end of the street. Standing beneath a light post, they resembled something nefarious.

"Listen closely. I told you I have a boyfriend."

"Who lets you walk home alone in the dark?"

"I'm a big girl, Paul."

"Luke."

"What?"

"I mean, *look*...just one drink. Can't hurt, can it?"

"Have you seen yourself? Besides, you already smell like a brewery. I'm not askin' again. Leave me alone."

"Dammit, Claud!"

He stared up at the moon, feeling as hideous as the

lunar surface. The rift between them grew wider, and he saw himself falling into it, hurtling towards the earth's belly.

"Hell is on earth," he said dramatically, staring at her full lips.

"You have problems."

"Yeah, I do. You."

"You insulting me, now?" Claudia asked, crossing her slim arms over her ample chest. "Way to win me over. Good night, Paul."

The vice clamped on his heart. He watched as she walked away, growing tinier. Like an inverted love song, he shouted his whisky-soaked words.

"Fuck you, Claud!"

Four

His sobriety was a self-induced punishment. Drool soaked his pillow. In his dreams, she came to him as a faceless entity exuding love. With fingers outstretched, she had refused to touch him until he pleaded with her and the sounds of his wails, filled his bedroom.

Cursing, Luke slammed his window shut to muffle the voices of the kids playing at afternoon recess. Being sober meant remembering. It meant that he could feel every emotion, just as he could feel the steely cold blade of a knife slicing through his flesh, deeper. Deeper. His scars were not symbolic of a battle won, or a demon slaughtered. They were simply, ugly -- and a reminder that there was no cure for his mental lesions. There was only remorse, and the sickening feeling that he was living the nightmare in his waking hours.

In the kitchen, he thought about the night's antics and the way he jumped out of Ricky's Chevy like a jacked up stuntman when he realized his cousin was driving towards the hospital psych ward. Luke had walked home, feeling the burn in his legs after an hour, talking to himself, thus giving credence to Ricky's diagnosis.

At the sink, he poured dark, oily, brew into his cup and filled the other half with whisky. Carrying it to the living room with trembling hands, he sat at the antique desk, and faced the Remington. Desperate to find solace in an imaginary world, he lovingly stroked the keys:

Where are you going?
To take a balloon ride way up high.
Why?
To catch the ghost that skirts the sky. To pull her down for one last kiss, then send her back to joy and bliss.

Luke lit a smoke and stared at the words – too gentle for a man on the brink of insanity. Downing the rest of his booze-laden coffee, he tried again:

The scent of jasmine perfume filled the air.
"Hurry, darling, we're going to be late."
"I have to put on my face."
"You've reapplied your lipstick a hundred times."
"Not that face," she said, dangling a leathery piece of epidermis between her fingers.

"Luke."

His smoke fell from his lips, burning his crotch. Squeezing his eyes shut, he prayed to Jesus that she'd have a face.

"Luke," Claudia repeated.

Swivelling in his chair, he faced his demons. She was flesh and blood. One arm was in a cast, just as it had been three years earlier when she fell from a ladder while decorating the house for Christmas, and despite the sadness that was painted across her cheeks, her lips no longer dripped venom.

"Claud..."

"I'm cold," she said.

"Baby, I…"

"What? Why are you looking at me weird?"

He glanced at the wall behind him as if Sane Luke would be standing there, ready to come to his rescue.

"I'm not looking at you weird."

"Did you pick up the hot dogs on your way home?"

"No," he said, approaching her like he would a Bengal Tiger. "I forgot."

"Christ. You know I can't cook with my stupid arm."

"I know. I thought we'd order a pizza," he said, wrapping his arms around her solid waist.

"Oh. That sounds good. Why is it so cold in here?" she asked, snuggling against him.

Luke pressed his lips against her head, wishing he

could superglue himself to her scalp. A phantom echo of what could have been reverberated endlessly, and when their eyes met, he caught a glimpse of the woman he married.

She shivered.

"Would you like a bath before dinner?"

"Yeah. Okay."

"Come on," he said, grasping her good hand.

At her touch, his insides quivered. The euphoria he felt was almost instant. He left his world behind for a different one void of misery, and pain, and summoning every ounce of courage, he banished the devil. This was a liaison for only two.

Guiding her on to the toilet, he filled the tub with hot water.

"As hot as you can."

"I know," he said, twisting his head towards her.

"How was work?"

"Same old shit," he lied, running his hand through the bath water. "How are you feeling, baby?" he asked, approaching her.

"Same. Tired. I still can't believe how stupid I am."

He had found her in agony, only minutes after her fall. Tinsel was threaded through her hair. She was like the angel that had fallen from the top of the tree.

Luke helped her to her feet, half-grinning, "You're not stupid. It was an accident. Let's get you warmed up."

She wore his white dress shirt, unbuttoned, and he struggled with her cast until she was freed from the sleeve. The black, silk, camisole she wore underneath was three sizes too big, and sliding the thin straps from her shoulders, he let the garment drop down the length of her body. Claudia stepped out of it like a dress. Naked, her nipples grew firm, and he bowed his head to lick one, and then the other, expecting his lips to stick like the time when he was a kid and French-kissed a steel pole in the middle of a deep freeze.

"Luke."

"What?"

"Later."

"Is it my fault that you're so beautiful?"

"Yeah, yeah."

He undressed her fully and led her to the tub. With a firm hold on her, she stepped inside, releasing an audible moan of pleasure.

"Too hot?"

"It's perfect," she said. With her eyes closed, she was lost in reverie.

Luke knelt beside her, enjoying the view. Picking up a washcloth, he lathered it with soap, and ran it across her back, her neck, her good arm, between her legs. His erection was painful.

"This feels so *good*."

"I'm glad baby, but I'm about to explode."

Claudia opened her eyes to see his bulge. They laughed in unison, bumping heads, and offering one another soft, innocent, kisses.

"What do you want on your pizza?"

"I don't care, as long as we can get half with anchovies."

"You're the only man I've ever met who likes anchovies on his pizza, Luciano," she told him, shaking her head. "What's going on with the new book? You haven't talked about it lately."

He smiled wistfully, racking his brain to remember what he was working on three years earlier.

Standing, he grabbed the bathroom cup to rinse her hair, and spoke to the mirror when he said, "It's coming along."

His reflection mocked him; shamed him.

"I don't feel so good."

He leaned on the wall between them, feeling the familiar tears sting his eyes.

"What's…what's wrong, baby?"

Plop.

"Claudia?"

Plop.

"Jesus Christ, not now. *Please!*"

He placed the cup down gingerly and went to her. A violent chill invaded his body. Dropping to his knees, he wept the tears that she could no longer spend for herself. Fishing with one hand, he retrieved two shrivelled grapes. Then his world went black.

Five

For Once in My Life was making Luke deaf. The proprietor of *Sell & Bye* played the record at increasingly mounting decibel levels. The lyrics stabbed at Luke's heart like a million tiny pinpricks letting what was left in it, bleed out.

"You hard of hearing?"

"What!?"

"Can you turn that damn thing down? And for Fuck's sake, can you tell me why it's spelled 'bye' and not 'buy' with a 'u'!?"

The man behind the counter sported salt and pepper hair, and a contrasting yellow beard. His hands were too small for his body, and, apparently, his ears were too. Reaching behind him, he lifted the needle from the record and faced Luke who was red-faced after lugging the 40-pound Remington from the parking lot to the front of the pawn shop where he engaged in a verbal showdown with the guy named Petey – according to his name tag.

"Well, Pete?"

"Petey. Well, what?"

"Why is it spelled, 'bye' with an 'e'!?"

"Because, jerk-off, when I buy it, you say, 'bye'."

"That's stupid."

"Wife's idea. What do you have for me?"

"You blind, too?"

Petey was not amused. His little sausage fingers drummed on the counter. "Listen, kid, you going to bust my balls all day? That hunk of junk ain't worth more than three bucks."

"Three fucking dollars?"

"It's missing the 'Q'."

Luke scanned the counter in front of him. Picking up a black leather-bound notebook, he tore a page from it and inserted it into the machine.

"Watch," Luke told Petey. "It still works."

QQQQQQQQQQQQQQQQQQQQQQQQQQQQQQQQQ
qqqqqqqqqqqqqqqqqqqqqqqqqqqqqqqqqqqqq

"See?"

"That's peculiar," Petey said, stroking his beard. "Still, it'll sit here gathering dust forever, and I have enough junk gathering dust. Two dollars and ninety-nine cents."

Luke clenched his fists, missing the feel of his wedding ring, "You're lowering your offer?"

"You stole a piece of paper. Two dollars and ninety-nine cents. Take it, or…bye."

"Clever, asshole."

A vulgar thought filled his head. His fingers inched towards the keys, and before Luke could send Petey into an ancient Gladiator arena, Mrs. Petey made an appearance.

"Phone's for you."

"Be right there. Just finishing up with this customer."

"You wish," Luke said, struggling to lift the magic relic into his scrawny arms. Teetering on his legs, he left the store and made it to his pick-up, dropping the typewriter into the passenger seat. Luke leaned over the steering wheel, swearing in both of his official languages.

Putting the truck in gear, he sped home, where he proceeded to bury the Remington in his backyard.

The next morning, Luke awoke with a mouthful of dirt, pebbles, and a plethora of fat, juicy, worms.

Six

Dear Claudia,

I vowed to love you "'til death do us part", but what if we could live together in death? ~~*What if I had the balls to let you die?*~~ *What if I joined you?*

"Anything else, love?"

The neon glow of five letters was unimaginative but the sign did its job inviting the haggard, hungry, and hobos inside. D-I-N-E-R.

Luke's three plates were wiped clean: Chicken Parmigiano with a side of silky spaghetti doused in homemade sauce, a double cheeseburger topped with caramelized onion, along with piping hot French Fries, and a mile-high, four cheese lasagna with a side of *Ollie's World Famous Garliest, Garlic Toast* that helped put the little diner on the map.

Luke turned his napkin over and stared up at the woman who resembled his aunt Rita when she was young, before the effects of too many cigarettes killed her looks. A lump caught in his throat, but despite the big red circle on his calendar, he opted not to leave a suicide note given that his family would spend the rest of their lives trying to analyze it and blaming themselves for every uncrossed "t" and every undotted "i".

"Just the bill, thanks."

"You got it," the waitress told him, smiling. "You must have a hollow leg."

"More like celebrating."

"Oh, yeah?" she asked, juggling three plates on her arm. "What's the occasion?"

"Going to meet my wife."

"She been away?"

"Something like that."

"Well, isn't that nice?" The waitress picked up Luke's love letter, scrunching it between her fingers.

"Wait! I'm…still using that."

"Sorry, love. Here you go," she said, handing it back to him. "Be right back with your bill."

"Thanks."

Washing down his Catholic guilt with a double whisky on ice, he scribbled his last words:

I'm kind of scared of God, to tell you the truth. What if He won't let me in to see you? You know what Ma always said about people who kill themselves: "Stuck somewhere between Heaven and hell. Stupid idiots." *This is hell, though, Claud. I'm already living in hell. How much worse can it get? Anyway, I'll see you soon.*

I love you,

Luke.

He was drenched the second he stepped outside. A torrential rain made the world look like a Dystopian version of itself, gritty and void of colour. A night silent; screams muted by the rain. The derelicts had sought refuge, while the madman was whistling a Broadway tune and walking leisurely towards the old fishing bridge that bordered town.

Luke left his pick-up at the diner. The keys were in the ignition, and on a different napkin, he had left the waitress her tip: *License plate: AYKE 987. Be sure to get an oil change as soon as possible.*

Unfettered by life's shackles, he was the star of his own show. He could see himself from another realm, and a likeness of his old self was cocooned somewhere else. They would find him, one day, between the pages of the book he never finished, or eternally smiling in his wedding picture. His life would be commemorated by a solemn ceremony.

Even Ricky would cry, and then stuff his face with food to sop up the tears.

Luke took notice of his surroundings. A fire hydrant was no longer an inanimate object, but a source of life. The graffiti with misspelled words was akin to art. A woman beneath an umbrella became a kindred spirit. The ethereal sounds of a saxophone were played in memoriam, but he was still alive; breathing, living, and using what little strength he had, he ran towards the bridge, visible in the distance, feeling euphoric.

Gasping for breath, he clutched the wood railing and looked at the angry waters below. The distance was too short. The water was too shallow. He swore out loud at the notion that he couldn't even kill himself properly. An intense feeling of anger bubbled up inside of him, and he sat, Indian style, engaging in futile attempts to light what he wished was his last cigarette, but the rain soaked the cancer-stick before he could pollute his lungs with it.

Standing, he walked to the other side of the bridge. Rocks were protruding from the earth where the water receded, and closing his eyes, he envisioned diving headfirst, and leaving his scrambled brains to dry in the morning sun.

"Paul?"

"Jesus."

"You planning to jump, or somethin'?"

"I…no. I'm doing research for my new book. What the fuck are you doing here?"

"Asshole Connor broke up with me. I made him pull over so I could get out!" she yelled over the rain.

"He…he broke up with you?"

"Yeah. Well, sort of. He asked if we could see other people. Told him to go fuck himself. He said he'd rather fuck Tammy Reynolds."

Luke tried to hide the smile spreading across his face, and as he moved closer to her, he could see that her smile matched his own.

"Does that mean you'll go out with me?"

"I have to," she said, "Wouldn't want your death on my conscience."

"I was doing research…"

"Yeah, yeah. You goin' to kiss me, or what?"

Luke moved forward and devoured her, unable to get enough – desperate to fill the gap left by her absence. Headlights allowed him to see her clearly. She was whole, wet, beautiful. His heart pounded in tandem with a car horn. He pushed her forcefully, out of the way of danger, and as she fell against the bridge, a rotted piece of wood gave way.

She lay with arms outstretched, reminiscent of Michelangelo's genius; rocks painted red.

Seven

"Mangia. Eat."

Luke sat in his mother's kitchen, picking at a piece of pancetta. She had found him sprawled on the couch, soaking wet, and crying in his sleep. In the morning, she lectured him about drinking too much, and how booze can make a person go blind. Her prescription included a hearty breakfast, orange juice squeezed by hand, and tiny cup, after cup of strong espresso.

"How you feeling?"

Luke shrugged, head bobbing like a drunkard. Her spatula met his shoulder. "I *asked,* how you feeling!?"

"Like shit."

"Don't swear! Why? What hurts? Where were you last night? *Almost gave me a heart attack this morning,"* she mumbled.

His headache intensified, stretching down his spine. "I was at the bar," he lied.

"Not the Nudie Bar, I hope?"

"No, Ma."

The sound of eggs cracking reminded him of his wife's skull splitting in half, and he wanted to vomit nature's goodness all over the fancy table doily.

"Why were you getting drunk? Is that why you walked here?"

"No. Truck got stolen."

"Stolen! Now, what? How are you going to work?"

Luke slammed his fork on the table, causing a mouse to scramble back into its hole, "Jesus, Ma, what's with all the questions? I'll figure it out, okay?"

Even with his back to her, Luke could see her heart breaking. He stood, and approached her, wrapping his arms around her aproned waist.

"I'm sorry, Ma."

"Forget it."

"No, look at me. I mean it. I'm sorry."

His mother faced him, and as if seeing him for the first time, she burst into tears. "You going to talk to me, now?"

He sought the counter for support. Leaning on it, he lit a smoke.

"It's…about a girl."

"What girl? You never talk about any girl. Come sit. My arthritis is acting up."

Luke sat back down, accepting the heavy crystal ashtray she handed him that once served as a milk dish for their dead cat, Christopher Columbus, a.k.a. CeeCee.

"What's her name? Do I know her? Luciano, do I know her mother?"

He saw a vision of the two proud mamas dancing at the reception, dressed head to toe in purple sequins.

"She...doesn't exist," he said, truthfully. "My heart is empty."

"Grazie a Dio. Thank the Lord. Is that all?" she asked, kissing her Madonna pendant. "You'll find her one day. I didn't meet your father until he was thirty-six. You're young, still. Almost thought your father was too old for kids. Like, dried up, if you know what I mean. Then we almost lost you."

"What?" he asked, suddenly coherent.

His mother rubbed her leg underneath the table, as if the gesture would rid her of the pain.

"Don't you remember? You were right here, at this very table. I think you were colouring and eating a peanut butter sandwich. I was outside hanging laundry but I had the window in the kitchen open so I could listen in case you called me. You started choking on that damn sandwich and pounded on the table, on account that you couldn't talk, or scream, or nothing. It sounded like an earthquake coming from inside the house. Thank God, I left the window open. I found you just in time. Anyway, you don't remember, do you?"

"No, I don't. Is that why you never bought peanut butter?"

"After that? How could I? Look," she said, standing, "I have to start new eggs. But have faith, *figlio mio,* she will come," she said, patting Luke's heart. "And when she does, you better not forget about me!"

"Thanks, Ma. I love you."

"I love you, too."

He snatched her wrist and squeezed it. "I really love you."

Nodding, she wobbled away.

Luke snuffed out his smoke. In the grey wisps left behind, he saw his future.

Eight

He smelled of Aqua Velva. *The cold stone floor beneath my naked back sent an icy chill up my spine. He placed his warm hand underneath me. The contrast of cold and warm intensified the sensation between my legs. His long hair fell over his eyes as he stared down at me. I kept waiting for him to say something. I wanted to hear my name, my nickname...anything. We could hear the voices of his co-workers in the main room where they worked the line. I couldn't breathe. I was afraid they would hear me. Luke's lips parted, but he still didn't speak. "Say something," I begged. He placed his finger to his lips to quiet me. The sun filtered through a window. I turned my head towards it, and closed my eyes, wanting to simply* feel *him. That familiar ache was followed by his normal rhythm. He released his breath in short gasps. My hands found him and forced him further into me. It was one of the many times that we stole time, and used it to connect with one another in a way that will forever be seared across my heart...*

Luke was on his hands and knees watering the dirt with his tears. His sobbing was endless, and he dug desperately to unearth the Remington that he had buried six feet under. He found her diary hidden in the furnace room as if a ghost child was at play, but her musings screamed "woman", and his heart bled all over the page.

Mud was smudged across his face from wiping at his dripping nose with dirty hands. A neighbour lady stared at him curiously, and he gave her a one-handed salute and continued digging like a deranged archaeologist. He heard the earth gurgle, regurgitating things that were meant to stay buried; forgotten. Excavating the machine with his bare hands, he likened himself to a doctor who had pulled a baby from its mother, soiled, and bloodied.

Inside the house, he dipped a toothbrush in whisky and scrubbed between the keys. Like ancient hieroglyphs, the letters held meaning that was far beyond him to transcribe. He was a wordsmith, pilfering consonants and vowels, attempting to make sense of the horror show that he had been thrust into unwillingly. He was like the cretin who goes and gets himself bludgeoned by the psychotic killer's weapon of choice, except the script wrote itself, and he – he was merely a player.

Luke stuck the toothbrush in his mouth and placed

an old record on the turntable. Along with Sinatra, he guzzled from the whisky bottle – taking one for the road. Walking dumbly around the house, he poked at picture frames until they were crooked. He rearranged the cups, glasses, and plates in the kitchen cupboard, and tossed her diary in the sink, lighting it on fire, melting her words. In the bedroom, he placed his pillow at the foot of the bed, moved his shirts to his underwear drawer, and using the booze bottle that was glued to his hand, he swallowed his wedding ring, and then hers.

Glancing at his watch, he counted the seconds as they ticked idly by, inching towards three. In some other universe, and with God as his witness, he had said "I do" at exactly three o'clock in the afternoon. God had become irrelevant. Time ceased to matter.

Sitting down, he turned on the desk lamp. It cast a soft light over his workspace, illuminating the Remington. Within its bowels, he could almost hear its heartbeat.

The pads of his fingers met the keys, and he stayed in that position, staring at the blank page, until he was overtaken by a desire so strong, it was as if he had relinquished his body to the devil. It was then, that he spoke out loud: "You were my favourite mistake."

His mother hummed a song from the Old Country. The wind licked at the sheets as she hung them on the line, and they waved in the breeze, obscuring her view. Inside, the little boy was bringing a purple chicken to life. He giggled as he imagined a real purple chicken and deciding the chick would look funnier with orange hair, he reached into the box with one hand.

With each keystroke, his breathing grew shallower.

The crayon broke between his fingers, and little Luke cried quietly, still munching on his peanut butter sandwich. The lump in his throat stopped the ball of bread and butter midway. He was unable to call for help. He was unable to breathe. With fists poised over the table, he froze before flesh could meet wood and

Books by Barbara Avon

Peter Travis Love Stories:

My Love is Deep

Briana's Bistro

The Christmas Ornament

The Christmas Miracle

A Two-Part Love/Time Travel Story:

Promise Me

Romance/Suspense/Time Travel:

STATIC

Timepiece

Windfall

Romance/Thriller:

The Gift

Michael's Choice

Horror:

The Simpleton

SPEED BUMP

Psychological Horror/Thriller:

Sacrilege

Paranormal Romance:

Postscript

Q.W.E.R.T.Y.

A Letter to Claudia

A Collection of Flash Fiction:

Love Bites

Love Still Bites

About the Author

Barbara Avon was born in Switzerland and immigrated to Canada when she was two years old. She grew up Italian in the Niagara Region and attended Notre Dame High School, and then Brock University. She moved to Ottawa, Ontario, in 1999 to pursue work. She has worked for two major Ottawa area magazines and is a published poet.

Always having had a penchant for the written word, she has dreamed of writing a novel. She is also the author of three unique children's books that allow the child to draw the illustrations, and a compilation of micro-fiction, "Love Bites." She is working on her next novel, a love story with her characteristic suspense element.

In 2018, she won SpillWords Author of the Month, as well as FACES Magazine "Favourite Female Author". She is an active member of the Writing Community on Twitter (@barb_avon).

Together with her husband, she has established BUCCILLI Publishing in homage to her maiden name.

Avon lives in Ontario, Canada with her husband Danny, their tarantula Betsy, and their houseplant, "Romeo".

An Excerpt from *"Timepiece"*

Available Now

1932

He was viciously afraid. The streets were deserted, save for the ones who were out to prey; searching for shiny trinkets, or money, like Wise Men who had lost their way.

Matthew walked with his hands clenching the inside lining of his overcoat pockets. Anna's face flashed across his eyes and he quietly berated himself for being less of a man. He had met her at tea, at the house of a mutual acquaintance, and was instantly entranced by her beauty. He had engaged her in conversation and soon learned that her high regard for modern advancements intrigued him as much as the shades of emerald in her eyes. Her parents had persuaded her to immigrate to Canada without them and she was lured by the promise of adventure. She had been coy with him at first, but quickly resigned her heart once he successfully showed her the extent of his own. A year later, they vowed all of their tomorrows to each other.

He felt immune to the bitter cold, welcoming it as a sort of punishment. He scanned the street before him, where, in the distance, a mutt sat tethered to a light post. Matthew walked towards it, with a simple destination in mind. As he drew near, a man materialized from an alleyway and crouched next to the canine, petting it.

Matthew met the two of them with the standard greeting, "Merry Christmas."

The man rose to his feet and adjusted his monocle. "Merry Christmas, kind sir. Do you always stroll the streets alone at twilight on the eve of our Lord's birth?"

Mathew raised his fedora from his tired eyes to better see the man whose girth was well hidden beneath layers of unfashionable cloaks. His vernacular was strange and mystified Matthew who could only think of Anna.

"I needed fresh air."

"Is that what you need?"

"Yes. Excuse me," Matthew said on his way past the man and his dog.

"Why don't you tell me what you really need, friend?"

Mathew slowly turned, curious to know the meaning behind the question. He studied the man's face which was plump and void of wrinkles, yet his moustache was long, and grey, and discoloured yellow.

The dog circled the man's legs incessantly.

"Sit down, Zeus, you're making me dizzy. Now," he said, turning his attention to Matthew, "what say you?"

"I already told you that I needed air."

"Air that you seek furthest from home?"

"How do you know where I live?"

"I don't. You just told me that I am correct in my assumption. My store is just down that way," he said, pointing towards the darkened alley.

Matthew felt his insides freeze. The man was a scoundrel, trying to lure innocents with Zeus.

"I'm not in need of any wares. Good night."

"I believe you are," the man said, seriously. "If you think I pose a threat, surely someone in your fine form could easily maneuver a man of my size? Come."

He unleashed Zeus from the light post and stood with his loyal dog by his side, waiting for Matthew to move. A gust of fierce winter air made Matthew lose his balance. The man with the monocle took the hint from nature and moved towards the alleyway. Unsure of himself, Matthew followed.

In the middle of the narrow pathway, they stopped in front of a door. The ancient sign on the wall was weathered and barely legible. Matthew stooped to read:

Enter, if you dare, my lair of incomprehensible delight.
Where madness prevails, and sadness dissipates upon entry.
A world where all your fantasies are within reach.
You need only state your peace.

"Is this a joke?" Matthew asked, standing.

The short man ignored him and unlocked the door. Zeus raced inside, seeking his bed that sat before a grand hearth.

Matthew's eyes adjusted so that he could see a large wooden table in the centre of the room, filled with trinkets old, and new. An apothecary's cabinet lined one stone wall, while a large black pot hung over the orange flames in the fireplace.

The man with the monocle lit a lamp and then a second and disrobed until his girth became but an illusion. He was scraggly, unlike his face.

"What's your name?"

"Henry."

"Henry what?"

"Just Henry. What is yours?"

"My name is Matthew Winters."

"Well, Matthew, tell me what it is you desire."

"I don't think I understand."

The little man waved his hand across the large table before him.

"What of it?"

Henry picked up a string of ladies' pearls. "See these? They look like a mere bauble. Yet, the woman who wore them could read people's minds."

Matthew's hearty laugh startled Zeus until the dog became bored and went back to sleep.

"You jest."

"Not at the moment, no. You see, Matthew, she had a suspicion. An ill-feeling, if you will. She had the notion that her husband was not being entirely faithful to her. She came to me for guidance. I gave her these."

Matthew stood with his arms crossed over his chest. The string of pearls was similar to the ones Anna has worn. His gaze shifted to Henry who was busy admiring the accoutrement.

"I suppose they didn't work?" Matthew stated, humouring the funny little man.

"Whatever do you mean?"

"She gave them back, it would seem."

"That's because she was finished with them. She didn't want to spend the rest of her life reading minds, Matthew. She had to pay a penance for returning them, though. Store policy."

Matthew's match stopped in mid-air. The cigarette between his lips quivered as he spoke.

"Penance?"

Henry's head bobbed up and down. "She can never love again."

Matthew's eyes narrowed at the tall tale. "Who *are* you?"

"I already told you. I'm..."

"Yes, yes. Henry, I know."

Matthew lit his cigarette, and unbuttoned his overcoat, slinging the garment over one arm. He walked around the space, feeling his host's eyes on his back. The room was long, and at one end, it was black and seemingly endless.

"What's down that way?" he asked, pointing into the void.

"That is where I sleep. Come now, Matthew, I'm sure you would like to get back home to your wife?"

His head spun, fast as lightning, "I didn't tell you that I'm married."

"You didn't have to. Your ring tells the story."

He looked down at his own hand, feeling foolish. He longed to hold her, and caress her hair, and feel the warmth of her body close to his. A torrent of memories washed over him. One particular day, while they were courting, his heart surged at the site of her. He had been shy the entire evening, prompting her to question his motives. He had tried to convince her that there was nothing but longing in his heart, but she refused to listen to such nonsense, until he fell to one knee.

"See this, my good man?"

Matthew focused his attention back to Henry who held his palm out. He walked back towards him, and crushed his cigarette out in a heavy, glass ashtray.

"Cuff links."

"Not just any cuff links. The wearer can endure affliction. The fellow who wore these felt no pain."

"What benefit was that to him?"

"Well you see, Matthew, he had a chronic illness and couldn't function in his daily life. These allowed him to live fruitfully."

Matthew stared at the cuff links. There was nothing extraordinary about them.

"What was his penance for returning them?"

"He died."

"You...murdered him?"

Henry laughed until his belly hurt, causing Zeus to snort.

"No, kind sir. He died of natural causes at the ripe old age of one-hundred-and-one. His widow was kind enough to return them to me. See this?" he asked, running his fingertips across a Remington typewriter.

"Yes, we use that model at the office."

"Well, this one is special, Matthew. This one makes everything you type come true. The elderly lady who owned it, wrote herself into a regal body, and surrounded herself with riches, and loyal subjects. She lost herself when the 'Q' stopped working, though. She was cast from her throne, and brought it back to me, demanding a refund."

Matthew's eyes scanned the wares, averting his eyes from the dwarfed shaman. There were various pieces of clothing, jewelry, books, and small household items.

"What does this do?" he asked, picking up a wristwatch.

"Ah, your instinct favours you today. That timepiece allows one to manipulate time."

"Manipulate it, *how*?"

"Surely you have read science-fiction novels. You

may use it to either go back, or forward in time. It's your preference. You need only state your peace," Henry said, reciting the line on the weathered sign. He looked weary and sat on a three-legged stool. Taking a handkerchief from his vest pocket, he removed his monocle, and wiped at his eyes.

"Are you all right?"

"Yes, yes. I am tired."

"Is your monocle a..."

Henry smiled. "You are wise, young Matthew. I have the privilege of living forever young, with the aid of this little gadget."

"But you just removed it. I saw you."

"It is still attached to my person," he told him, lightly tugging at the wire.

"How old are you?"

"Twenty-eight years old."

"No. I mean, when were you born?"

"The year of our war."

"*Which* war, Henry?"

"The War of 1812."

Matthew threw the wristwatch on the table and slammed his hand on the wooden surface before him, making it smart. The funny man leaned far back on his stool, attempting to escape the onslaught of words.

"What kind of charlatan are you? Do you expect me to believe all of this? Why, a child has a better imagination! I don't know what kind of joint this is, but I'm done with the fairy tale. You...you quack! Have a Merry Christmas."

He swung his overcoat over his shoulders, and turned hastily towards the door, cringing at the sound of Zeus's howl.

"I can prove myself to you, Matthew, if it's evidence that you seek. Perhaps a cup of cheer?"

He turned to see Henry shuffle his way towards the apothecary cabinet. He opened the glass door and pulled a bottle from it, along with two crystal tumblers, and shuffled his way back to Matthew who wore a permanent scowl. Henry placed the bottle and glasses on the table and picked up the watch. He handed it to his disgruntled guest.

"Put it on," he said in a tone unlike his other. He busied himself by pouring bourbon into each glass.

Matthew observed the gold timepiece. Its face was dressed in roman numerals. It was slightly heavy, but otherwise, unassuming. Once he was satisfied, he placed it on his wrist.

"How was your drink?"

"What drink?"

One empty glass sat before him, and Matthew could

taste the sticky sweet pleasure of alcohol on his lips. He stumbled backwards, ignoring the merriment on Henry's face.

"What just happened?" he said, raising his hands before him as if staving off an opponent.

"What happened, is that you stated your peace. It seems as if you desire going into the future. Is that accurate? It will take a little getting used to. You don't remember the bourbon, as it was your first time connecting with the artifact. You'll remember everything else."

Instinctively, Matthew attempted to rid himself of the evil by removing the watch.

"Stop! It's imperative that you never take it off. It runs on your heartbeat, Matthew. Do not ever let it stop ticking."

"I haven't a choice, now?"

"No. But I think that secretly pleases you," Henry stated victoriously. He drank from his own tumbler and smacked his lips together. His moustache wiggled with delight.

Matthew leaned on the table, desperate for answers.

"How does it work? What about Anna? Where can we go, Henry? You must tell me!"

"Your enthusiasm is refreshing."

Matthew caressed the watch as if it were alive. "I haven't any money..."

"It is free of charge."

"But why?"

"It is free of charge on one condition."

"What might that be?"

Henry adjusted his devil's eye. "That if you ignore my instructions, you agree to the consequences."

"My penance."

"Yes."

"What is my penance?"

A long silence ensued. They both listened as a group of carollers made their way past the shop. The air inside thickened. Matthew could feel the sweat moisten his back. Henry seemed content and surprised them both when he said: "It is unimportant, so long as you keep that mechanism on your wrist. You may take Anna with you. She must be in agreement, and she must hold your hand when you both decide to leave. You must both abandon this time in your hearts, as well as your minds. Wear nondescript clothing. Remember that you can not tell anyone."

"We simply disappear?"

"In a sense. You will not disappear, but your friends and family must think you did."

"Can it harm her in any way? The trip, I mean."

Henry smiled at the man's chosen words.

"Not in any alien sense. She may be emotionally affected, until she, too, gets used to it."

Matthew lit another nervous smoke and offered one to Henry.

"I quit smoking ninety years ago. But thank you, kind sir."

"Can we come back? Can we ever come back?"

"That would be a negative. Therefore, you must make careful decisions. You can only go into the future at this point. Never backwards. Once you choose your time, it will pass in a linear fashion, just like now."

Matthew paced back and forth in front of the table. Zeus followed him with his eyes. He stopped, suddenly, and allowed anxiety to replace excitement.

"But where will we end up? Where do we live?"

"Simply imagine it."

"That's all?"

"Yes."

"What if it gets wet?"

"It is resistant to water damage. You may bathe with it. Now, Matthew, I must say my prayers and rest my weary head," he said, getting to his feet. *"My eyes have seen too much,"* he whispered.

"Yes, of course. But please, Henry. You must tell me how this all came to be."

"I wish I could," he stated sadly, "but I do not know. My great great-grandfather was proprietor of this shop. It simply changed hands through generations. You can imagine my disorientation. I was thrust here before my time. A young man, unsure of the world's wicked ways. I longed to live forever. To outlast evil and witness good again."

An angry wind rattled a windowpane. Zeus whimpered. The burning embers were dying and cast a rosy hue over the mangy mutt. Matthew looked at the time. It was just past midnight, and somewhere, a Church choir sang an ode to baby Jesus.

"Does the watch tell proper time?"

"Yes. It works."

"But not in the future."

"It will work according to the time and day that you land. I am tired, friend. Why do you stand there?"

Matthew pulled his overcoat from his shoulders and put it on. "I'm afraid," he stated, bluntly.

"I would worry if you were not. To fear the unknown is natural. Why do you wish to go to the future, Matthew? Most people would like to go to the past. Somewhere familiar."

He felt as if he were standing on the edge of a pirate's plank, and only Arturo could save him, but the man was drowning in a sea of his own.

"I wish to escape my troubles," he confessed.

Henry nodded, "I can relate. The imagination is a powerful thing, friend. Use it with caution, or you may find yourself in a heap of trouble."

Matthew's thumbnail met his mouth, "What happens if I go astray, Henry?"

"The answer is bleak.

"In what sense? *In what sense, bleak?*"

"In a manner that would be of no use, should you be privy to the details."

"What if..."

Henry's smile lines deepened, "Come now, Matthew. Consider it an adventure. Go, and be well."

The two men stared at each other, intent on memorizing every intimate detail. Matthew extended his hand towards the little man, who took it and shook it vigorously.

"I will show you out," Henry said, walking around the wooden table and towards the front door. He paused with his skeletal hand on the doorknob.

"Remember all that I have told you."

"Yes. Thank you, Henry. I don't know what magic this is that you purvey, but I feel like it was fate, that I found you this evening. Good night."

Henry merely nodded and opened the door. His guest tipped his hat at him and disappeared amidst a heavy snowfall.

He used all of his remaining strength to push the door closed against the whistling wind, secured it, and picking up one lamp, walked with it towards the void.

"Come, Zeus."

The candle cast a soft light over a single bed, a nightstand, a small bookshelf lined with Bibles, and several of Zeus's pillows that were strewn across the floor.

Henry sat on the side of his bed and rubbed his loyal companion behind the ears.

"Sleep well, old boy," he told him, releasing him.

The dog walked in three circles, before collapsing into a cloud of pillows. Henry washed his hands in a basin, removed his earthly clothing, extinguished the lamp, and climbed underneath the sheets. He stared into the blackness and prayed to Satan.

"I have paid my dues. I'm coming home, father," he whispered.

The monocle fell to the floor.

Zeus yawned.

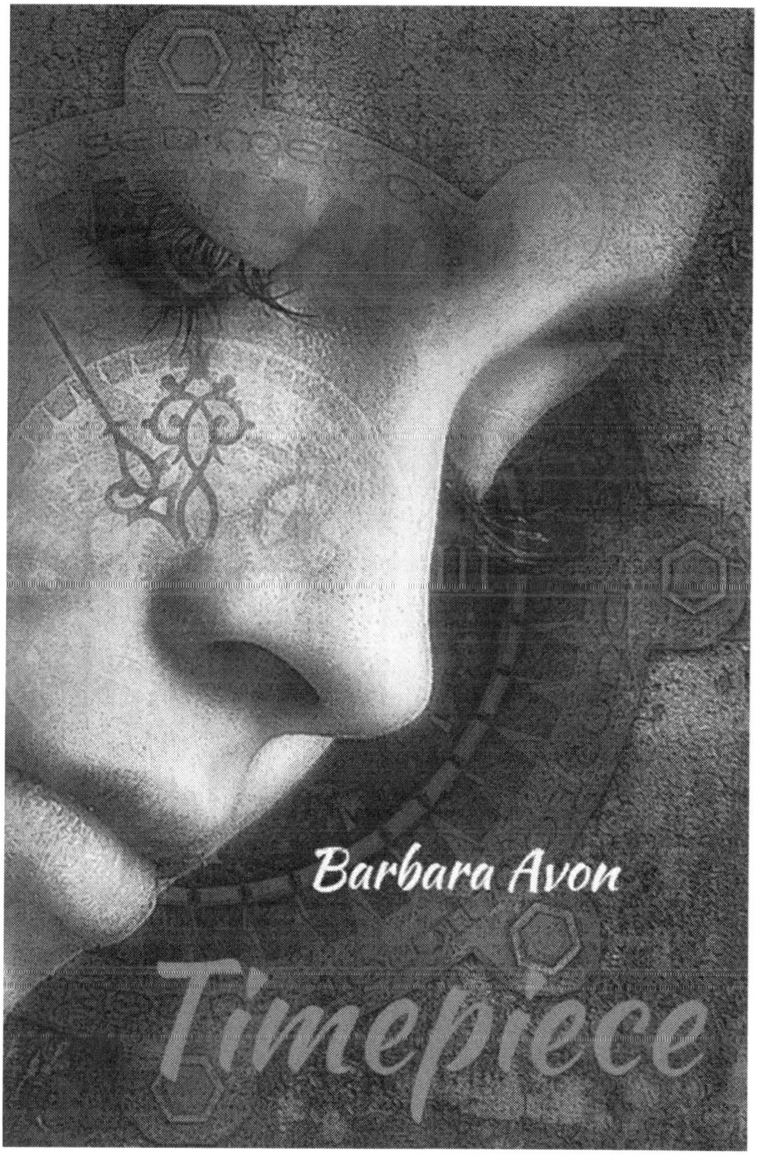
Barbara Avon
Timepiece

Printed in Great Britain
by Amazon